# MySELF Bookshelf

# We Are Brothers

Written by DaYun Oh

Illustrated by Anna Godeassi

Language Arts Consultant: Joy Cowley

NORWOOD HOUSE PRESS

Chicago, Illinois

## DEAR CAREGIVER

**MySELF Bookshelf** is a series of books that support children's social emotional learning. SEL has been proven to promote not only the development of self-awareness, responsibility, and positive relationships, but also academic achievement.

Current research reveals that the part of the brain that manages emotion is directly connected to the part of the brain that is used in cognitive tasks, such as: problem solving, logic, reasoning, and critical thinking—all of which are at the heart of learning.

SEL is also directly linked to what are referred to as 21st Century Skills: collaboration, communication, creativity, and critical thinking. MySELF Bookshelf offers an early start that will help children build the competencies for success in school and life.

In these delightful books, young children practice early reading skills while learning how to manage their own feelings and how to be considerate of other perspectives. Each book focuses on aspects of SEL that help children develop social competence that will benefit them in their relationships with others as well as in their school success. The charming characters in the stories model positive traits such as: responsibility, goal setting, determination, patience, and celebrating differences. At the end of each story, you will find a letter that highlights the positive traits and an activity or discussion to help your child apply SEL to his or her own life.

Above all, the most important part of the reading experience is to have fun and enjoy it!

Sincerely,

*Shannon Cannon*

Shannon Cannon, Ph.D.
Literacy and SEL Consultant

Norwood House Press • P.O. Box 316598 • Chicago, Illinois 60631
For more information about Norwood House Press please visit our website at www.norwoodhousepress.com or call 866-565-2900.

Shannon Cannon – Literacy and SEL Consultant
Joy Cowley – English Language Arts Consultant
Mary Lindeen – Consulting Editor

**Library of Congress Cataloging-in-Publication Data**
   Oh, DaYun.
    We are brothers / by DaYun Oh ; illustrated by Anna Godeassi.
      pages cm. -- (MySelf bookshelf)
    Summary: "Having a brother can be tough. Little Brother does not always want to share his toys and
    sometimes starts a fight. Big Brother gets in trouble for not setting a good example and sometimes
    has to sit in the thinking chair. Despite it being tough, Big Brother and Little Brother realize having a
    brother can be fun"-- Provided by publisher.
    ISBN 978-1-59953-657-6 (library edition : alk. paper) -- ISBN 978-1-60357-717-5 (ebook)
    [1. Brothers--Fiction.]  I. Godeassi, Anna, illustrator. II. Title.
    PZ7.1.O4We 2015
    [E]--dc23
                                        2014030348

Manufactured in the United States of America in Stevens Point, Wisconsin.
263N—122014

I was playing with my little brother.
We were playing a game with robots.
My robot was old. His robot was new.
"Yee-hah!" we yelled. Bang, bang, bang!

Daddy shouted at us, "Quiet, boys!
Go to your room!"

COLD sea

6

I said to my little brother,
"Let's change robots."

He hid his robot behind his back.

"I just want to play with yours one time,"
I said, reaching for his new toy.

He yelled, "Dad! Dad!
He's trying to take my robot!"

Dad came in, angry with me.
"You go and sit in the thinking chair!"

Dad doesn't know anything.
I just wanted to play
with the new toy.

8

I would be very happy
if I lived in a house full of toys.
Everything would be mine!
Every day would be like my birthday.

I decided to ignore my brother.
I stared at the TV, but he began to giggle.

I tried to get the remote
so I could change the channel.

"No!" he said. "I want to watch this!"
He sat on the remote
and stuck his tongue out at me.

When I pushed him away
and grabbed the remote,
he started to cry.

Mommy rushed in,
and my little brother ran to her.
He was crying loudly.
Mommy said to me,
"You are the big brother.
Why did you hit him?"

"I didn't hit him!" I said.
"I just pushed him."

But Mommy said, "You go and sit
in the thinking chair."

13

Mommy doesn't know anything.
She doesn't know how angry
I am to be the big brother.

14

If I was a clear jellyfish,
no one would see me.
I would eat my brother's ice cream.
I would push him and poke him.
No one would know
I was his big brother.

15

Dinner time was a silent battle.
I stared at my little brother.
He stared back at me.
I pushed his chair.
He pushed my chair.
When I touched his dish,
he touched my dish.
Tap, tap, tap-tap-tap!

I stood up and shouted at him.
"You are such a jerk!"

Mommy and Daddy got mad at me.
"What's wrong with you today?"

"Why do you always blame me?" I yelled.
"You don't know anything!"

So here I am, in the thinking chair.
I'm the one who always gets punished.
I'd like to go away and be anywhere but here.

20

I wish I could fly like a bird in this chair.
I'd fly so high in my chair that
I would not be able to see my house.
I would not be able to see my little brother.

But then I hear my brother calling me. He is saying, "Why are you on that chair all by yourself?"

22

I stop dreaming.
My little brother has a dining chair.
He is pulling it over beside me.
"What are you doing?" I ask.

"I want to be with you," he says.

He and I have a late dinner.
"Did you cry?" he asks.

"No," I say.

"You did so," he says.

"I did not!"

"Yes, you did! You did!"

And, so we are at it again!

Dear Little Brother,

I'm sorry for calling you names.
We were having fun playing with robots together,
and then it turned into a big fight. I'm not sure how that happened.

Sometimes it feels like Mom and Dad take your side and that they love you more. That is why I get mad at you sometimes, even though I really like you.

If anyone else ever picked on you, I would run to protect you and help you. We are a team. But when we are at home with Mom and Dad, sometimes I feel like you are my enemy. We compete with each other to get toys or the TV remote or attention from Mom and Dad.

But even then, we are still brothers. You will always be my baby brother, and I will always be your big brother.
I will always love you!

With love from,
Your big brother

# SOCIAL AND EMOTIONAL LEARNING FOCUS
## Coping with Sibling Conflicts

If you have siblings, you know how big brother feels. You might feel jealous of a sibling, because it can seem like they get more attention. Remember, if they are younger, they may need more help from grown-ups than you do.

If you are the oldest, it might help to remember that your younger sibling probably looks up to you and is jealous of all the things you can do. You can be a role model to your siblings by setting a good example and controlling your emotions, even when they really upset you.

In the story, the older brother was sent to the thinking chair. He felt punished, but the chair is a good place to cool off and think about how to make things better. You can find a place that helps you think—it doesn't have to be a chair, it could be a special place all your own. If each sibling chooses a special place, others will know that, when they are there, it is important to leave them alone to sort out their feelings.

Make a sign to place near your special space. You can use the example shown here to get started. Be sure to include a few ideas of the things you will think about when you are in your space. For example, things that make you happy, what you might say to make things better, something fun you can do with your sibling.

When the younger brother brought a chair to be near big brother, it gave them a chance to realize that they really do love each other. You can have your own "talking chairs" to help you and a parent or sibling talk about what is bothering you and come up with a solution together. Instead of feeling punished, the talking chairs help you share your feelings and listen to those of others.

Try this too ... *(continued on next page)*

This is **My** Special Place.

When I am here, I like to think about:

- playing fetch with my dog
- saying I am sorry when I do something bad
- sharing my toys with my brother

On a piece of paper you and your siblings can make lists of things that each of you likes or can do. Use the example below for ideas.

Things the brothers in the story can do to get along:

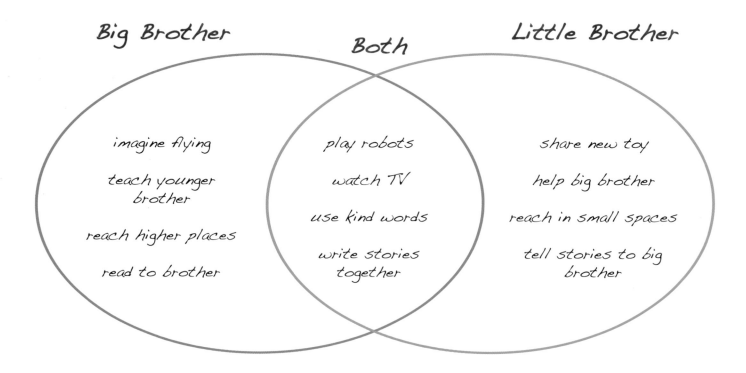

Big Brother

Both

Little Brother

*imagine flying*

*teach younger brother*

*reach higher places*

*read to brother*

*play robots*

*watch TV*

*use kind words*

*write stories together*

*share new toy*

*help big brother*

*reach in small spaces*

*tell stories to big brother*

# Reader's Theater

Reader's Theater is an interactive approach to reading that allows students to understand each story through dramatic interpretation. By involving students in reading, listening, and speaking activities, they provide an integrated approach for students to develop fluency and comprehension. A Reader's Theater edition of this book is available online. You can access the script by scanning the QR code to the right or visit our website at:
http://www.norwoodhousepress.com/wearebrothers.aspx

# The Happiest Season of All

## HOLLY POND HILL

### ILLUSTRATED BY SUSAN WHEELER

#### Written by Paul Kortepeter

HARVEST HOUSE PUBLISHERS

Eugene, Oregon

# THE HAPPIEST SEASON OF ALL

Text Copyright © 2001 by Susan Wheeler
Published by Harvest House Publishers
Eugene, OR 97402

Library of Congress Cataloging-in-Publication Data

Wheeler, Susan, illustrator.
    The happiest  season of all / Susan Wheeler; text by Paul Kortepeter.
        p. cm. —
    ISBN 0-7369-0505-7
        1. Christmas. 2. Christmas decorations. 3. Christmas cookery. I. Kortepeter, P.F. (Paul F.), 1959-
    II. Title. III. Series.

GT4985 W465 2001
394.2663—dc21

2001016902

Design and production by Garborg Design Works, Minneapolis, Minnesota

Scripture quotations are from the Holy Bible, New International Version®. Copyright © 1973,
1978, 1984 by the International Bible Society. Used by permission of Zondervan Publishing
House.

**For all the merry days,**

*thanks Mom and Dad.*

**Paul**

**The artwork in this book is dedicated to Abbie and Papa Joe, my sweet Mark, Matthew, Rodney, Mikie, Kimmie, Murray, Buster, Mason, Julie, Joey, Jenna, and Jakie. I can't imagine Christmas without all of you...**

*I love you all dearly!!!*

**Suskie**

# Contents

# INTRODUCTION

## Joy to the World

Our hearts they hold all Christmas dear,
And earth seems sweet and heaven seems near.
—MARJORIE PICKHALL

Christmas has come again to Holly Pond Hill. As I sit in the bay window upstairs, I can see lights gleaming all over town. The birdhouses are aglow with candles as they sway on evergreen branches and the squirrels have hung lanterns high from their nests in the trees. Luminaries line the cobbled streets downtown and the shadows of evening shoppers hurry from baker to milliner to haberdasher.

How I love this time of year when every sensation seems enchanted! The scent of pine garlands mingles in the air with the aroma of sugar cookies, fresh from the oven. Outside, a sharp gust of wind sends up a spindrift, causing snow crystals and stars to dance together in the shimmering sky. From afar I can hear the voices of carolers singing *Glorias* and *Fa-la-las* to each other across the frozen hills. And here, in hand, is a cup of hot mulled cider, sending wisps of steam across the pages of my journal. If only I could capture these delights in a bottle—to be uncorked throughout the year—I would be the cheeriest of all rabbits!

I love the contrasts of Christmastime. Yes, it can be frightfully cold, even for rabbits who never go without a coat of fur. But despite the cold, the season positively glows with warmth. A crackling fire and a steaming hot bath are the perfect accompaniments to snow and ice. How I enjoy the familiar hiss of the radiator and the feel of a hot water bottle under my blanket. The colder it is without, the cozier it is within.

It is also so very dark at Christmastime. The sun seems no sooner to rise than it sets again. And yet how bright

Christmas stands against the satiny background of December's black nights! Light pours from carriages and shop windows, from tiny candles and towering trees. Brightest of all are the faces of children as they look with wonder at each new splendor.

Christmas is a busy time, filled with noise and bustle. One can hardly walk about the Village Green without bumping into a brass band or crowds of revelers. And yet, for those who seek it, a deep peace pervades the season. Peace can be found in the hush of a new fallen snow or in the quiet contemplation of a dying fire. It can be found in the strains of "Silent Night" and in the fellowship of a candle-lighting service. Above all, peace can be found in remembering the coming of the Savior to the world, in pondering how He redeems each day with His love.

Christmas is all these things—cold and warm, dark and bright, noisy and still. And inside of me there exists a contrast as

well. During Christmas, I am only half grown-up. The other half of me is still a child—eyes full of wonder, heart full of joy.

The carolers are strolling down the path to my house now. Every step they take toward my front door, "Joy to the World" grows louder and brighter. I must hurry to greet them with mugs of sugarplum punch. Joy to the world indeed!

*Victoria Rose Boxwood*

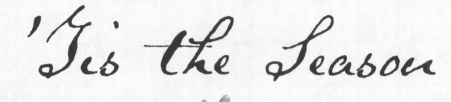

# 'Tis the Season

## WELCOMING
## THE HOLIDAYS

Now thrice welcome, Christmas,
Which brings us good cheer!

—POOR ROBIN'S ALMANACK (1695)

Before Yuletide can properly begin, Hannah Nibbler inevitably goes on a tirade against the whole season. Her annual grousing has practically become a Christmas tradition.

"By my cottontail, I can't wait for the holidays to be done with," she said to Elizabeth Stubblefield and me one wintry day. We rabbit ladies were together at my home, Boxwood Meadows, wiring holly garlands for the village lampposts. "So much fuss and bother and rushing about! We civilized rabbits practically trample each other on the way to the cash register. And let's not forget the Christmas music. By the tenth of December, I've heard every carol at least a million times. Even Theodore, the turtle taxi, torments me with 'Silver Bells' as he drives from shop to shop. I tell you, it's enough to make Charles Dickens weep."

Elizabeth has a difficult time letting any slight against Christmas go unanswered. "Wasn't it Charles Dickens who said, 'I will honor Christmas in my heart, and try to keep it all the year'?"

"Goodness gracious—all year!" Hannah protested. "If I had to keep Christmas all year, I'd out-scrooge Scrooge himself!"

Now Hannah's complaints are fairly familiar. I don't know anyone who is completely immune to the sundry irritations of the holidays. Surrounded by crowds of shoppers, by glittering lights and ear-numbing music, we may believe we don't have a merry bone left in our bodies.

I think, however, Christmas is best kept at one's own pace. At home, I can set the tone for enjoying the holidays. If I desire a festive parlor, I'll light every candle on the tree. If I'd rather sit quietly and read a book, I'll light a single scented candle. This morning I wanted to listen to some jazzy carols, so I turned on the gramophone. Last night I let silence reign and listened instead to the sleet rattling on the windowpane. Feelings of joy and goodwill don't seem so out of reach when I'm away from all the hoopla.

O Tannenbaum,
O Tannenbaum,
How lovely are your branches!

10

I have also observed that the haste of the holidays adds in no small measure to the season's grouching. To put it plainly, we are too busy.

I know of some rabbits who prepare for Christmas the way they would prepare for a wedding. There are guests to invite, cards to send, feasts to prepare, halls to deck, gifts to wrap, stockings to stuff, and new outfits to wear. On top of that, there are shows to catch, trees to cut, galas to attend, ornaments to create, puddings to steam, mountains to ski, and skates to sharpen. My dear friends, this is too much! It is not possible to plan a wedding every year and not dread weddings! So, too, for Christmas.

My pastor, Rev. Josiah Sunday, gave me some much-needed insight for keeping a healthy perspective on Christmas activities. "Victoria Rose," he told me, "Christmas will come in all its glory whether we lift a finger or not. The good Lord's stable had naught for decoration but bales of hay and a bright star. Yet it was the loveliest spot in the universe. 'Let every heart prepare Him room.' That's all we really need to do."

> But give me holly, bold and jolly,
> Honest, prickly, shining holly;
> Pluck me holly leaf and berry
> For the day when I make merry.
> —CHRISTINA ROSSETTI

For me, the secret to enjoying Christmas year after year is to celebrate Advent, a church observance dating back to the fourth century. It is a time to reflect on Christ's coming to the manger. It is also a time to look forward to His second coming some glorious day in the future. The word *Advent* itself is derived from the Latin *adventus*, which means "coming" or "arrival."

Once I remember that Advent is a time for reflection and preparation, then everything else falls into place. I prepare for Christmas by opening my life to heavenly insights. I prepare by turning away from injurious attitudes. I mend friendships; I ask for forgiveness; I love my family more tenderly. Advent is also a time for me to lend a helping hand to those important charities that strengthen the weaker members of society. When my heart is too hectic, it has little room for making peace or for spreading goodwill.

Well before the holidays, I gather my family together with calendar in hand. We talk about the essentials of the season—the Christmas Eve pageant, Aunt Drusilla's sleigh-ride party, holiday

baking—and we mark these on the calendar in red. We also set aside several days with nothing scheduled at all. These are reserved for rest and family time. After that, we use a green marker to fill up the calendar with other things we'd like to do if time permits—ice sculpture contests, madrigals at the Tea Room, the *Nutcracker* ballet. We won't let these events crowd out the peace of the season should life get too busy.

Our family calendar caught my eye as Hannah Nibbler continued to wax negative about the season. "Have you ever tasted anything so horrible as fruitcake with hard sauce?" she asked. "If it weren't for tradition, I'd never touch the stuff. What were our fore-mothers thinking when they made the first Christmas fruitcake? Surely they could have come up with something more appetizing, like cherry cheesecake or peach cobbler."

"Hannah," I said (rather too firmly), "I am going to add your annual feast of complaints to my calendar. You will always find me a ready listener on that day. But I am going to have to restrict you to one day only, and the earlier in the season the better."

Well, I'm afraid that took the wind

out of her sails. She fell silent and her ears drooped a little. We rabbit ladies resumed our holly wiring in silence.

Finally I said, "Dear Hannah, was there ever a time that you loved Christmas?"

"Oh, yes," she sighed. "When I was a child."

"What did you love best?"

"The Christmas lights reflecting on the snow, I think…" Her eyes took on a faraway look, as if she were gazing at something in the distance of her memory. "I loved watching the snowflakes dance around the old spruce tree in our front yard, bright from top to bottom with blue lights. The whole family would gather around it on Christmas day and sing 'O Tannenbaum.'" She shook her head. "How strange to think that I once loved Christmas *and* snow."

Elizabeth gave me a wink. "It's snowing outside now."

"Yes," Hannah sighed again. "I shall

have to shovel the sidewalk."

I leapt to my feet. "Last one out is a rotten egg!" Elizabeth and I grabbed our coats and a branch of holly and bounded out the door. Hannah sat there at the table in utter bewilderment—for a moment only. Then she charged out the door after us. We three ladies went skipping down the street, waving our branches and kicking up the snow.

Poor Hannah! She had forgotten that the notion of growing up is foreign to Christmas. At Christmas, the Savior Himself became a child. When we take time to recapture our first love for the season, and to prepare our hearts for the coming King, how much more we will welcome Christmas!

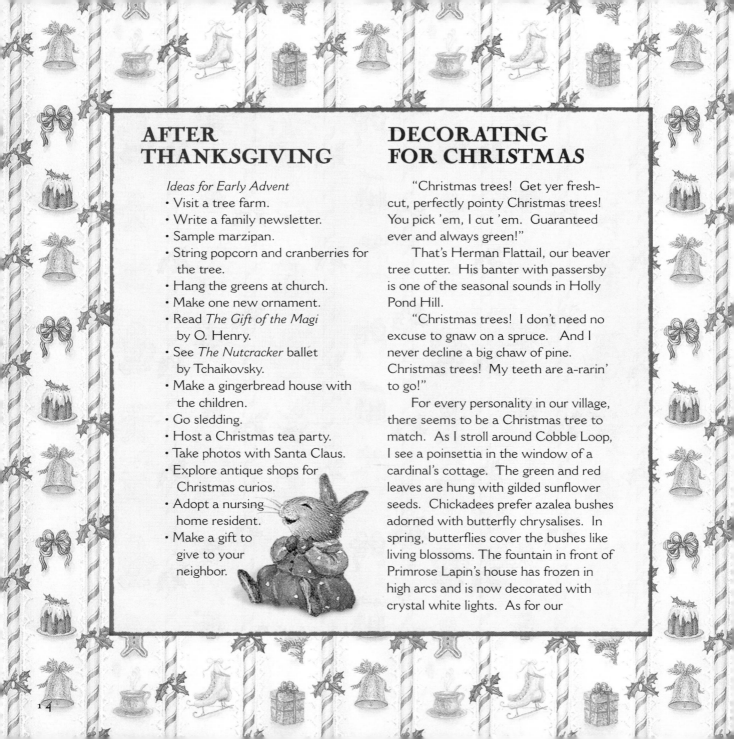

## AFTER THANKSGIVING

*Ideas for Early Advent*
- Visit a tree farm.
- Write a family newsletter.
- Sample marzipan.
- String popcorn and cranberries for the tree.
- Hang the greens at church.
- Make one new ornament.
- Read *The Gift of the Magi* by O. Henry.
- See *The Nutcracker* ballet by Tchaikovsky.
- Make a gingerbread house with the children.
- Go sledding.
- Host a Christmas tea party.
- Take photos with Santa Claus.
- Explore antique shops for Christmas curios.
- Adopt a nursing home resident.
- Make a gift to give to your neighbor.

## DECORATING FOR CHRISTMAS

"Christmas trees! Get yer fresh-cut, perfectly pointy Christmas trees! You pick 'em, I cut 'em. Guaranteed ever and always green!"

That's Herman Flattail, our beaver tree cutter. His banter with passersby is one of the seasonal sounds in Holly Pond Hill.

"Christmas trees! I don't need no excuse to gnaw on a spruce. And I never decline a big chaw of pine. Christmas trees! My teeth are a-rarin' to go!"

For every personality in our village, there seems to be a Christmas tree to match. As I stroll around Cobble Loop, I see a poinsettia in the window of a cardinal's cottage. The green and red leaves are hung with gilded sunflower seeds. Chickadees prefer azalea bushes adorned with butterfly chrysalises. In spring, butterflies cover the bushes like living blossoms. The fountain in front of Primrose Lapin's house has frozen in high arcs and is now decorated with crystal white lights. As for our

CHRISTMAS
TREES
·FOR SALE·
YOU PICK 'EM
WE CUT 'EM

Susan
Wheeler

15

porcupine mayor, Zach Stickleback, his tree is bedecked with icicles and prickly snowflakes.

Wreaths adorn many a front door. They are the simplest of all holiday decorations, yet they tell passersby that the spirit of Christmas lives within. Chipmunks hang walnut wreaths on their cottages and then consume them on Christmas Day. Mice weave string cheese together until they form cheese hoops. By December 25, the cheese wreaths are thoroughly nibbled and tattered!

Materials of an endless variety may be used in the making of a wreath: pine branches, reindeer moss, bittersweet, eucalyptus, magnolia, red peppers, candy, dried apples, ivy, brambles, roses, paper fans, Christmas cards, teddy bears, and chestnuts, to name just a few.

My favorite Christmas decorations, of course, are the most personal. They are often ornaments that carry some special meaning, like the gingerbread paw print made by my daughter Emily in Bunnygarten. Or the glass heart given to me by my husband, Edmund, our first Christmas together.

Every year I'll hang miniature picture frames from our tree. The frames contain the portraits of family members from near and far. Even though we can't always be together for Christmas, these family portraits impart a strong sense of togetherness.

Another favorite decorating tradition comes on Christmas Eve. Each member of my family writes a little love letter to every other member. Then we roll the letters into scrolls and hang them on the tree with ribbons. Before we open our stockings, we read the letters aloud.

The special ornaments of a family give each tree its distinction. No two trees are ever exactly alike. Each tree magically takes on the personality of the family who adopts it.

# ADVENT WREATH

### The true light that gives light to every man was coming into the world.

JOHN 1:9

Advent wreaths are a wonderful way to keep Christ at the heart of Christmas. They are easy to make and, like a crèche, they give a spiritual focus to holiday trimmings.

The wreath is a circle symbolizing God's unending love. Four candles stand up in the greenery and a new candle is lit every Sunday in Advent. Traditionally, three of the candles are purple (a color of repentance) and one of the candles is rose or pink (colors of joy). A family devotional can mark the lighting of each candle. In the center of the wreath, place a stocky white candle, the Christ candle, for burning all Christmas Day.

• Many craft stores and Christian bookstores sell Advent wreath sets.

**Be merry all,**
**Be merry all,**
**With holly dress**
**the festive hall;**
**Prepare the song,**
**The feast, the ball,**
**To welcome merry**
**Christmas.**
**—W. R. SPENCER**

The craft stores also carry wire and straw molds, artificial garlands, and silk ivy, for making a wreath at home. (Avoid Styrofoam molds because they tend to fall apart with repeated use.)

• Evergreens are a beautiful symbol of eternal life. A pine garland from a tree farm is probably the easiest way to wrap fresh greenery around a wreath mold. Otherwise, you can simply attach uniform tree stems, about 5" long, one at a time with wire. Once the wreath is covered with greenery, prune back the stems to make a uniform circle. Decorate with ribbon or sprigs of holly and ivy.

• Securely anchor the candleholders. Tipping candles and fresh greenery can be a fire hazard.

# ADVENT DEVOTIONALS

## First Sunday –
## The Candle of Prophecy

Read Isaiah 9:2-7 and Isaiah 40:1-11.

*The first purple candle is lit.*

**Songs:** "Come, Thou Long Expected Jesus" and "O Come, O Come, Emmanuel."

**Classic Prayer**

Lord Jesus, Master of both the light and the darkness, send Your Holy Spirit upon our preparations for Christmas. We who have so much to do seek quiet spaces to hear Your voice each day. We who are anxious over many things look forward to Your coming among us. We who are blessed in so many ways long for the complete joy of Your kingdom. We whose hearts are heavy seek the joy of Your presence. We are Your people, walking in darkness, yet seeking the light. To You we say, "Come, Lord Jesus!" Amen.

—Henri J. M. Nouwen

## Second Sunday –
## The Bethlehem Candle

Read Micah 5:1-5 and Luke 1:26-38.

*The first and second purple candles are lit.*

**Song:** "O Little Town of Bethlehem" (Read the fourth stanza as a prayer.)

**Classic Prayer**

O holy child of Bethlehem,
Descend to us, we pray;
Cast out our sin, and enter in,
Be born in us today.
We hear the Christmas angels
The great glad tidings tell;
O come to us, abide in us,
Our Lord Emmanuel.
  —Phillips Brooks

## Third Sunday –
## The Shepherd Candle

Read Luke 2:1-20.

*The first and second purple candles and the rose candle are lit.*

**Songs:** "The First Noel" and "While Shepherds Watched Their Flocks."

**Classic Prayer**

O Father, may that holy Star
Grow every year more bright,
And send its glorious beam afar
To fill the world with light.
—William Cullen Bryant

## FOURTH SUNDAY –
## The Angel Candle

Read John 1:1-14.

*The three purple candles and the rose candle are lit.*

**Songs:** "Angels We Have Heard on High" and "It Came upon the Midnight Clear."

**Classic Prayer**

Dear Lord, as the angels proclaimed on the night of Your birth, "Glory to God in the highest," we too rejoice in the gift of Your precious Son. Help us to prepare our hearts to receive Him and joyfully share the wonders of His love.
—Author Unknown

## CHRISTMAS DAY –
## The Christ Candle

*Replace the purple and rose candles with white candles.*

Read Revelation 21:1-7.

*All candles are lit.*

**Songs:** "Joy to the World" and "O Come, All Ye Faithful."

**Classic Prayer**

Loving Father, help us remember the birth of Jesus, that we may share in the song of angels, the gladness of the shepherds, and the worship of the wise men. Close the door of hate, and open the door of love all over the world. Let kindness come with every gift and good desires with every greeting. Deliver us from evil by the blessing which Christ brings, and teach us to be merry with clear hearts.
May the Christmas morning make us happy to be Thy children, and the Christmas evening bring us to our beds with grateful thoughts, forgiving and forgiven, for Jesus' sake. Amen!
—Robert Louis Stevenson

# MUGS OF MIRTH

When the winter wind nips at your nose, these two steamy drinks are sure to warm you down to your toes. To keep drinks warm after preparing them on the stove, pour them into a slow cooker set on low.

## YULETIDE PUNCH

1 bottle (48 ounces) cranberry juice cocktail
1 can (46 ounces) unsweetened pineapple juice
2 cups water
1/4 cup firmly packed brown sugar
2 tablespoons fresh lemon or lime juice
2 teaspoons whole cloves
4 sticks cinnamon bark

In a large saucepan, combine all ingredients. Heat all ingredients on a medium setting until very hot, but not boiling. Simmer on a low setting for 15 minutes, stirring occasionally. Strain and serve. (To avoid the step of straining, spices may be placed in a cheesecloth bag.)

## HOT SPICED TOMATO JUICE

1 can (46 ounces) tomato juice
2 tablespoons butter
2 teaspoons Worcestershire sauce
1/2 teaspoon prepared horseradish
1/2 teaspoon dried oregano leaves
1/4 teaspoon hot pepper sauce
Salt and pepper to taste
Garnish of fresh chopped cilantro

In a large saucepan, combine all ingredients except cilantro. Heat on medium setting, stirring occasionally, until very hot but not boiling. Serve immediately with garnish.

# SWINGIN' AROUND THE CHRISTMAS TREE

Strange as it may seem for a rabbit with Victorian tastes, I can think of no better music to welcome the holidays than some buoyant jazz. As soon as there's a nip in the air, the old chestnuts start to dance in my head: "Cool Yule" by Louis Armstrong and the Commanders, "Winter Weather" by the Benny Goodman Orchestra and Peggy Lee, "Jingle Bells" by Duke Ellington, and "Winter Wonderland" by Ella Fitzgerald.

Many of the catchy pop tunes that are today considered classics first came out during the big-band or swing era of the 1930s and '40s. The lilting style of the day lent itself to secular rather than sacred sentiments. Some of the tunes, like "White Christmas," got their start in the movies, while others, such as "Santa Claus Is Coming to Town," were first introduced on the radio. It's in the early part of the season that I most enjoy jazzy pop music. As Christmas Day approaches, I find myself drawn to the more reverential carols.

When holiday music appears on the shelves, hurry out to find the tunes of the big-band era. Some good compilations exist and almost every major orchestra back then recorded at least a few holiday singles. Don't neglect the zesty crooners of the day either: Frank Sinatra, Billie Holiday, Nat King Cole, and, of course, the voice of Christmas, Bing Crosby.

# Oliver's Poetry CORNER

## PLEASE, CLOUDS, SNOW

Please, clouds, snow,
Don't say no!
One flake blowing by…

Way up high,
What's this I spy?
Two flakes flying by…

Oh boy, it's a flurry!
The world's all blurry,
Sparkles of white
scurry by…

Yikes, it's a blizzard,
And I'm getting frizzard,
Zillions of flakes
whizzing by…
—Good bye!

22

**Dear Primrose,**

I am considering a unique approach to Christmas colors this year. I am thinking of decorating in fuchsia and canary yellow, though I fancy tangerine and hot pink as well. I can't decide which color combination will create the biggest sensation with my neighbors. Would you kindly help me make up my mind?

Sincerely,
Simply Smashing

**Dear Simply Clashing,**

The colors you mention are perfect--if you plan to spend Christmas on the beach in Hawaii.

I don't know that creating a scandal—er, excuse me, sensation—should be the goal of your Christmas decorating. Christmas is a time to preserve tradition, which gives us a sense of belonging to each other and to the past.

Traditional Christmas colors tend to contrast with the earthy tones of winter without seeming unnatural. Green and red come to us from the leaves and berries of the holly bush, which creates welcome islands of color in landscapes of brown and white. Holly green blends beautifully with the greens of pine and fir trees.

Deep blues and purples are also traditional Christmas colors. The deep blue of the winter sky summons up images of the heavens over the nativity. Purple is a royal color, signifying the kingship of Christ. Both blue and purple tend to create a cool impression, especially when combined with silver.

For a warmer feel, I would suggest red and gold. Of course, the association of gold with Christmas comes down to us from the Wise Man who made a gift of gold to the Christ child. This precious metal splendidly complements the wooden floors, trim, and furniture of many homes.

Finally, gold or silver can be combined with snow white for the most formal, elegant look of all.

Keep the traditions, my friend. They are what make us feel the most at home.

Meticulously yours,
Primrose Lapin

# Draw 'Round the Fire

## MAKING HEARTS READY

Heap on more wood!—the wind is chill;
But let it whistle as it will
We'll keep our Christmas merry still.
—Sir Walter Scott

What a joy it is to step outside and take a deep breath of winter air! The cold somehow clarifies every odor and makes the nose more keen. Often the breeze will carry the delicious smoke of pine logs or the hint of mince pies. Just now the air is laden with the smell of roasting apples. My neighbors are singing the "Cabbage Head Carol" (for rabbits would never sing about boars' heads) as lazy gray smoke drifts from their chimney through the birch trees:

> "The cabbage head in hand
>     bear we,
> Bedecked with bays and broccoli."

I see the smoke rising from my own chimney and the sight fills me with warmth even before I return to the fireside.

The hearth has long been a metaphor for family affection. A fire in the home has the power to gather family members together and hold them spellbound with its flaming colors, its flashing shadows, its hisses and pops. The winter can never be too cold and dreary where a fire blazes merrily.

Besides the hearth, the "home fires" in my family are constantly burning in the kitchen. My oven is hardly ever cool. At no time during the year is our kitchen so much the center of activity as at Christmas. Friends and neighbors gather around our old stove to stave off the chill, to lend a hand, and to watch for some treat to emerge.

Baking is one of the Christmas pastimes that truly brings my family together. Emily and Oliver have more fun assisting me in the kitchen than they do playing with their tops and rocking horses. Each one of us has an important job to do:

chopping nuts, measuring flour, buttering pans, cutting cookies, and licking spoons. Even my youngest, Violet, can stir the batter.

Yes, it's true that the corner grocer carries cookie dough and cake mixes— and the village bakery opens at the crack of dawn. Yet I wouldn't trade family baking time for all the convenience food in the world. Baking is a wonderful opportunity to work together as a family. When so many activities seem to pull us in separate directions, baking together gives us a common labor. It is the times of hard work and shared purpose that we remember most fondly as we look back at childhood.

Baking and cooking also impart tradition to our children. The food we make from scratch often reflects our family heritage. I remem-

ber last Christmas how my daughter rescued a cherished tradition. Nine-year-old Emily was baking cookies for our annual cookie exchange party. My teacakes were cooling and I was relaxing in the parlor, playing checkers with eight-year-old Oliver. Dreamy smells flowed out of the kitchen.

"Mom," said Oliver, "I'm fainting with hunger. I haven't had a bite to eat since my last snack."

"You just finished a bowl of cheese popcorn," I reminded him.

"Oh dear, I'm afraid I must be growing again. Do you think that Emily is in a generous mood? ''Tis the season of kindling the genial fire of charity in the heart.' So says Washington Irving."

"My advice is wait until tonight, Ollie. Then you may eat to your heart's content."

Heedless of my good advice, Oliver stood up and staggered to the kitchen door. Doubled over, he knocked urgently. "Emily, dear sister," he groaned, "I'm wracked with hunger." He was only half playacting; the other half of him was quite sincere. "Dear sweet kind nice good unstinting…"

*Unstinting?* I thought. The smell was truly irresistible, and somehow familiar, though I couldn't place it.

"…pretty clever kind sweet pretty

happy loving gentle sister," he said. "It's me, Oliver, your favorite and only brother."

To my surprise, Emily opened the door with a big grin on her face. She held a plate in hand. "One for you and one for Mom," she said. "But tell me honestly what you think."

Oliver devoured his treat before I could cross the room. "If I had stopped to taste it," he said, "I would say that it was scrumptious. Any more?"

"Nana's chocolate madeleines!" I exclaimed. "Wherever did you find this recipe? I've been looking for it since before you were born!"

As it turns out, Emily had discovered the recipe card in the dim recesses of the pantry. It had been lost for years and now it was found—the same madeleines that my mother made and my grandmother before her. I felt as though we had rescued a priceless antique misplaced for years.

When my youngsters leave home, I intend to send them forth with a binder filled with our family's favorite recipes. Recipes should be treated with ample respect, like treasured heirlooms to be passed from generation to generation. They are every bit as much a part of our family inheritance as are the books we read and the memories we share.

# A CHRISTMAS COOKIE EXCHANGE

Christmas cookies come in such vast array that they easily outnumber the possible baking days in Yuletide. One way to sample a fair number of cookies, while gathering together dear friends, is to host a Christmas cookie exchange. For this type of party, guests bring a plate of homemade cookies to share along with the recipe. Once all guests are assembled, have them sit around the fire and take turns recounting their favorite Christmas tradition or memory. After this storytelling time, encourage guests to mingle over hot drinks and seasonal treats. Before they leave, your guests should fill up a plate of Christmas cookies, taking a few of every kind. You'll also want to provide paper and pens for guests to copy any recipes they would like to try later. Send your friends home with a cookie ornament or a cookie cutter as a memento of the party.

**He has more to do than the ovens in England at Christmas.**
—ITALIAN PROVERB

# KEEPING CHRISTMAS

*Ideas for the High Holidays*

- Replace linen sheets with flannel.
- Call an old friend.
- Make popcorn balls.
- Go cross-country skiing.
- Take a hot bubble bath.
- Read Dickens's *A Christmas Carol.*
- Attend a performance of Bach's *Christmas Oratorio.*
- Browse window displays with motorized toys and trains.
- Host a caroling party.
- Roast chestnuts.
- Stay overnight at a Christmasy bed-and-breakfast.
- Tarry under the mistletoe.
- Throw a family slumber party around the Christmas tree.
- Cut out paper snowflakes with your children.
- Have your children place a pair of shoes outside their bedrooms the night before Saint Nicholas Day (December 6). Fill shoes with chocolate money, shortbread, dried fruit, and nuts.
- Support Project Angel Tree or the Salvation Army.
- Make homemade Christmas cards with your children.

# THE COOKIES OF CHRISTMAS

What makes a cookie a Christmas cookie? How did gingerbread or pfeffernüsse gain such a distinction? I should think that any festive cookie reserved exclusively for the season probably qualifies. Some ordinary cookies, like shortbread and sugar, also fit the bill if they are cut into holiday shapes or brightened by glaze and sprinkles.

The cookies listed here are some of my absolute favorites, cookies I return to year after year. A tin of these cookies, delivered to friends and neighbors, is certain to spread holiday cheer.

SusanWheeler

29

## THUMBPRINT COOKIES

*These popular cookies are rich and nutty, but not too sweet.*

> 1 cup softened butter
> 1/2 cup brown sugar
> 2 eggs, separated
> 1 teaspoon vanilla extract
> 2 cups flour
> 1/4 teaspoon salt
> 1 1/2 cups finely chopped walnuts
> Currant jelly or other fruit jelly

- Preheat oven to 375° F.
- In a medium bowl mix all ingredients together except for egg whites, walnuts, and jelly. Reserve egg whites in a small bowl and walnuts in another bowl.
- Beat egg whites until foamy.
- Roll cookie dough into 1-inch balls. Dip each dough ball into the beaten egg whites.
- Next roll dough balls in finely chopped walnuts until walnuts are clinging to every side.
- Place balls 1 inch apart on a baking sheet. Bake 5 minutes at 375° F.
- Remove cookies from oven and press thumb into the center of each. Return cookies to oven and bake 8 minutes longer.
- Cool cookies. Fill thumbprint with currant, cherry, or mixed-fruit jelly.

**The Christmas fires brightly beam
And dance among the holly boughs,
The Christmas pudding's spicy steam
With fragrance fills the house,
While merry grows each friendly soul
Over the foaming wassail bowl.**
—ANNE FIELD

## LINZER SQUARES

*These layered bars, half tart and half cookie, are a luscious, jammy treat. They are similar to the Austrian linzertorte, but minus the time-consuming lattice top.*

### Cookie layer

> 3/4 cup all-purpose flour
> 3 tablespoons granulated sugar
> 1/4 teaspoon salt
> 6 tablespoons chilled butter
> 2 tablespoons finely chopped almonds, blanched and toasted
> 1/2 teaspoon vanilla extract
> 1/2 teaspoon almond extract

### Jam layer
2/3 cup seedless raspberry or
strawberry jam

### Finishing touches
3 tablespoons butter, room
temperature
6 tablespoons confectioners' sugar
1/2 cup finely chopped almonds,
blanched and toasted
1 egg, lightly beaten

- Blanched (skinless) almonds are available at the grocer's. To blanch almonds at home, place them in a heat-resistant bowl and pour boiling water over them. Soak almonds for a minute, drain water, and remove skins. To heighten flavor and restore crispness, spread almonds in a single layer on a baking sheet and toast in a 325° F oven for 10-15 minutes. Watch for a light browning and then remove quickly from heat. Dry almonds from the store need only be toasted for about 7 minutes. Chop toasted almonds finely.
- Prepare the cookie layer by mixing together the flour, sugar, and salt. Slice the chilled butter into manageable squares and then cut it into the flour until the texture of the dough is similar to that of cornmeal. Mix in almonds and extracts. Spread cookie dough evenly across an ungreased 8-inch square pan.
- Spread jam evenly over the cookie layer.
- Preheat oven to 350° F.
- Now prepare the icing layer. In a medium bowl, cream the butter. Add the confectioners' sugar and salt to the butter and beat until fluffy. Spread the icing lightly over the jam, taking care to disturb the jam layer as little as possible. The icing will melt more evenly once in the oven.
- Lastly, sprinkle the chopped almonds evenly over the icing.
- Bake for 30 minutes, or until the icing is a golden brown.
- Cut into bars while the torte is still slightly warm.
- Serve at room temperature. These freeze nicely.

*If only all I ever ate,*
*Were tarts of raspberry by the plate,*
*With gooey middles, red and sweet,*
*And flaky crusts, a buttery treat,*
*Why then I'd feel just like a king,*
*And never eat another thing.*
—OLIVER

## CRESCENT COOKIES

*These cookies are so light and buttery they practically melt in your mouth. The conspicuous taste of almond and the festive crescent shape give them their character.*

1/2 pound (2 sticks) butter
3/4 cup confectioners' sugar
2 cups flour
1 cup finely ground almonds
1 teaspoon almond extract
1/2 teaspoon vanilla extract
3/4 cup confectioners' sugar for coating

- Preheat oven to 300° F.
- Cream butter. Stir in sugar, flour, nuts, and extracts of almond and vanilla. Mix dough well.
- Form dough into delicate, finger-thick crescents, about two inches long. Roll crescents in confectioners' sugar and bake on ungreased cookie sheets for 12 minutes, more or less. Crescents should be set, but only very lightly browned.
- Cool crescents on cookie sheet. Roll crescents gently in the confectioners' sugar again. After this second coating, they are ready to eat.

## ENGLISH TOFFEE

*The toffee in this holiday favorite is sandwiched between chocolate and nuts. Be sure you have a candy thermometer before you get started.*

1 cup finely chopped pecans or almonds
24 ounces semisweet chocolate
1 cup unsalted butter
4 tablespoons water
1 teaspoon vanilla extract
1 cup light brown sugar

- Coat a 7 x 11 pan with butter. Spread 1/2 cup chopped nuts evenly in pan, reserving the other 1/2 cup.
- Melt 12 ounces (half) of the chocolate, either in the microwave or in the top of a double boiler. Reserve the other 12 ounces. Spread the melted chocolate over the nuts in pan.
- To make butter toffee layer, melt butter

## MOCHA BARS

*These mouthwatering brownies taste equally of chocolate and coffee. What a treat!*

1 1/2 cups all-purpose flour
1 teaspoon baking powder
1/4 teaspoon salt
1 1/2 sticks butter, softened
3/4 cup granulated sugar
1 cup dark brown sugar
2 eggs
2 teaspoons vanilla extract
2 tablespoons instant decaffeinated coffee dissolved in 2 tablespoons hot water
1 cup chocolate chips

over low heat in a medium saucepan. Stir in water, vanilla, and sugar. Turn heat up to medium and stir occasionally while the temperature rises. Cook the candy mixture until the candy thermometer registers 290° F, just above the "soft crack" level. Continue to cook for three minutes or so, stirring frequently, until mixture turns golden brown. Immediately pour over chocolate and spread evenly. Toffee hardens quickly!

- Melt remaining 12 ounces of chocolate and spread over toffee. Sprinkle remaining chopped nuts over chocolate.
- Cool completely and break into pieces to serve.

- In a medium bowl, combine flour, baking powder, and salt.
- In a large mixing bowl, cream butter. Add granulated and brown sugar and mix well. Add eggs, coffee, and vanilla and mix again.
- Blend dry ingredients into butter and sugar mixture.
- Fold in chocolate chips.
- Spread mixture into greased 9 x 13 pan. Bake at 350° F for 30 to 40 minutes. Cool completely before cutting.

# Oliver's Poetry CORNER

## GINGERBREAD FOR CHRISTMAS

Gingerbread boys, must you bake
   so slow?
I 'bout died of hunger an hour
   ago;
I 've waited so long for a boy of
   my years,
I 've got aches in my back and
   knots in my ears.

The stove fills the air with spicy-
   sweet smells,
That jingle my nose like the
   ringing of bells,
And my eyes, they 're a-pleadin'
   for a taste of this treat,
For a taste I can smell way down
   to my feet.

How I wish I 'd made linzers or
   tassies or tarts,
Sweet shortbread sandies with red
   jelly hearts,
A poor pfeffernüsse would ne' er
   be this naughty,
Neither would brownies nor
   orange biscotti.

O cookies for Christmas, how
   long must you take?
The seconds drag on and still you
   won' t bake!
I 've waited all year for you dear
   gingerbreads,
To dip you in milk and bite off
   your heads!

**Dear Primrose,**

I come from a family of well-bred rabbits. Perhaps I should say well-breeding rabbits. In any case, I have so many brothers and sisters, nieces and nephews, that the gift giving leaves me well nigh penniless every time we celebrate. This year I am thinking of feigning pink ear and avoiding the gathering altogether. Have you any advice before I run my thermometer under hot water?

Sincerely,
Sadly Lacking

**Dear Sadly Slacking,**

You may feign pink ear one year, but what about next year? Radish tummy? No, dear reader, it is best to avoid exile and share your predicament honestly with family. Unless you come from a long line of spendthrifts, you may find that others welcome the discussion.

One option is to draw names for gifts. Well before Christmas Day, the hostess can ask all participants to send her a list of gift ideas within a set price range. The hostess then pairs names at random, mailing gift lists to designated givers. Everyone in the family, from youngest to oldest, can participate in the name drawing. In the end, you will receive one gift only, but at least it will be something you want.

Some families are such inveterate gift givers that it may be impossible to wean them from piles of packages. In such cases, one gift per household might be the way to go. Why not create a specialty homemade treat? Wrapped creatively, a tin of cookies or a jar of spiced pickles make sensational gifts. These days anything homemade is sure to amaze and astound overworked relatives.

Don't neglect gifts of personal service either. Volunteer yourself as a baby-sitter—pass out coupons good for one night of absolutely free time off.

If all else fails, simply show up at your family festivities empty handed. Someone is bound to take pity and share a bite of plum pudding with you.

Meticulously yours,
Primrose Lapin

# THE SCENTS OF CHRISTMAS

During Christmas, the first sensation to greet visitors at the door is often the smells wafting from inside. When rich aromas from the kitchen mingle with the fresh scent of evergreens, the air itself gives a warm welcome that lingers long after the smells fade from awareness. Deeper layers of scent can emanate from candles, pomander balls, and potpourri, all combining to make a home as richly perfumed as a royal palace.

There is no secret to making pomanders or potpourri, except that they both take time to cure. Both start with natural ingredients that are pleasantly aromatic. These natural smells tend to fade after a week or so, but they can be enlivened time and again with a light sprinkling of essential oils, available at health, craft, and cosmetic stores.

## POMANDERS

- Choose fruit with an aromatic rind, such as oranges, lemons, or apples. Pierce the rind gently all over with a toothpick or a small nail, taking care not to tear it.
- Insert whole cloves into the punctures, close together, until the fruit is thoroughly studded.
- Roll the fruit in a mixture (equal parts) of these ground spices: cinnamon, cloves, nutmeg, and allspice.
- Hang the pomander with ribbon in a warm, dry place (such as a closet), allowing it to dry for a week. If the atmosphere is too moist, the pomander will rot rather than dry.
- Some Christmasy oils to consider adding to the pomander include clove, apple, pine, sandalwood,

cinnamon, and lemon verbena. Be parsimonious, however, as these essences are powerful.

## POTPOURRI

The word *potpourri* means "rotted pot" in French. Despite the unfortunate name, a bowl of potpourri in the house can blend with the festive atmosphere to make a sensational memory. For ingredients, consider both durability and visual appeal. Dried flowers and flower petals are potpourri staples, as are citrus peels, cedar shavings, and whole spices. Evergreen cones, sprigs, and needles will create a northern look while acorns, beechnuts, and dried leaves will create a more temperate look.

• Mix ground spices together in equal parts: cinnamon, nutmeg, clove, and allspice. For a single bowl of potpourri, one tablespoon of each spice should do the trick.
• Stir the spice mixture into the base of natural ingredients. Add a few drops of a favorite essential oil.
• Allow the potpourri to cure in an airtight container for a month or two, shaking occasionally to complete the blending of aromas.

# WASSAIL

Wassail or "waes hael" is actually a centuries-old toast in Saxon English. It literally means "be whole" or "be healthy." The correct reply to "waes hael" is "drinkhael," or "your health (as well)." In the olden times, young stalwarts in a parish would carry a wassail bowl door to door and sing at each house. The householders would add to the bowl some steaming wassail from their own stove. Our tradition of Christmas caroling comes partly from these rowdy wassailing parties.

There are a good many drink recipes these days that pass for wassail, or lamb's wool as it was called in the Middle Ages. Here are two alternative cider punches for your wassailing party.

## WINTER WASSAIL

2 cups granulated or light brown
   sugar
1 quart water
2 teaspoons whole cloves
4 sticks cinnamon bark
2 tablespoons fresh chopped
   gingerroot

1/4 teaspoon ground allspice
2 quarts apple cider
3 cups pulpy orange juice
3 cups lemon juice

- In a Dutch oven or large saucepan, stir sugar into water and bring the mixture to a boil. Boil uncovered for 10 minutes until syrupy. Remove from heat.
- Add spices to the hot sugar syrup and cover. Let stand in a warm place for 1 hour.
- Strain the syrup to remove the spices. Add apple cider, orange juice, and lemon juice to the clarified mixture. Bring wassail quickly to boiling. Serve piping hot. Keep warm in a slow cooker.

## HEARTY WASSAIL

1 gallon apple cider
2 cups unsweetened pineapple juice
1 tablespoon whole cloves
1 tablespoon whole allspice
4 cinnamon sticks
1/2 teaspoon ground mace
1/4 teaspoon fresh chopped
   gingerroot

1/4 teaspoon grated nutmeg
1/4 teaspoon salt
Dark brown sugar, to taste
2 lemons
2 oranges

- In a Dutch oven or large saucepan, combine cider, pineapple juice, spices, and salt. Bring the mixture to a rolling boil. Reduce heat, cover the pan, and simmer for 15 minutes.
- Remove wassail from stove and strain, discarding spices.

- While still warm, add brown sugar to taste.
- At this point, wassail may be refrigerated for later use. Otherwise, pour into a slow cooker on high setting.
- Slice lemons and oranges thinly. Add fruit slices to wassail and allow them to simmer for 30 minutes. Reduce heat to low setting. Water may be added if wassail becomes too concentrated. Serve warm.

# SING, CHOIRS OF ANGELS

I love Christmas carols for their poetry. They are nearly as delightful to read as to sing. No music is so closely linked with the celebration of Christmas as carols. The earliest carols derive from the sacred chants of the medieval church as well as Celtic dances called *caroles*.

Many early carols were originally sung in Latin, the universal language of the Roman church, or they mixed Latin with the common language, such as English or French.

"Angels We Have Heard on High" and "The Boar's Head Carol" are two examples of intermingled Latin and English. "Veni Emmanuel" ("O Come, O Come, Emmanuel") is our oldest surviving carol and dates back to the twelfth century.

Few choral works can rival the

exhilaration of Benjamin Britten's *A Ceremony of Carols*, composed in 1942. Britten combines the poetry of medieval and Renaissance carols with contemporary music. Incredibly, the work sounds ancient and modern at the same time. The composition has many different moods, from the sweet lullaby "Balulalow" to the joyous climax "Deo Gracias."

I close my eyes during the opening "Procession," a plainsong chant, and imagine myself swallowed up in a huge Gothic cathedral. The *Ceremony* ends with a recessional. This type of walking chant, poetry in motion, is how carols got started in church in the first place. If ever the traditional carols grow a little ho-hum, Britten's *A Ceremony of Carols* is sure to quicken one's pulse.

# O Holy Night

# ENJOYING THE WONDER OF CHRISTMAS EVE

Then be ye glad, good people,
This night of all the year,
And light ye up your candles:
His star is shining near.

—AUTHOR UNKNOWN

Of all the nights in all the year, Christmas Eve is the most wondrous. It is a night set like a diamond within a golden wreath of carols.

In Holly Pond Hill, there is no feasting or playing games on Christmas Eve, no dancing or revelry. The entire village makes its way to the outdoor theater for a pageant about the Christmas story. There, as the snow falls gently around us, we hear again the rich passages from the Gospels of Luke and Matthew recounting the birth of Jesus.

I remember one Christmas Eve when Oliver was to perform as a shepherd boy and Emily was to play the part of Mary. We bundled the children in festive attire and Edmund lit the candle lantern. Oliver pulled baby Violet along on his favorite sled.

As the family made its way down the snowy lane, we passed through a copse of evergreens. Suddenly a delivery sparrow landed on a branch overhead, sending down a shower of snow. It dropped a telegram into Edmund's hands and chirped "Urgent! Urgent!" before flying off again.

Edmund scanned the note. With a

> Love came down at Christmas,
> Love all lovely, Love Divine;
> Love was born at Christmas;
> Star and angels gave the sign.
> —Christina Rossetti

sigh, he folded it into his pocket. "Little Basil Butternut has taken a turn for the worse. He's running a high fever."

As a country doctor, Edmund must frequently make house calls at the worst possible times. Often he takes his leave in the middle of dinner or in the middle of the night and sometimes during a raging blizzard. I could see the disappointment in the faces of our children.

"But Papa, you won't get to hear me recite the Magnificat," Emily said.

"And what about my line?" Oliver asked. He cleared his throat. "And there were in the same country shepherds abiding in the field, keeping watch over their flock by night…"

"That's just it Oliver and Emily," Edmund said. "I have to be like those watchful shepherds sometimes. My

heart to falter in the line of duty. A tear glistened in his eye, as if a snowflake had melted there.

This was too much for Emily. "When you take care of Basil," she piped up, "pretend you're taking care of the baby Jesus. That way you can feel a little bit like you're part of the pageant."

Edmund knelt down in the snow and hugged the children. "My wise Emily. That's just what I'll do. I'll treat Basil just the way I would treat the baby Jesus."

Edmund stood up and hurried away through the woods. As the rest of us continued toward the theater, I pondered the exchange there among the trees. Jesus did say, "Whatever you did for one of the least of these brothers of mine, you did for me." In a real sense we do take part in the Christmas story every time we bless someone with our love. Truly it is Christmas every time we let God love others through us.

And this is why Christmas Eve is the most wondrous night of the year. We remember the Gift beyond measure that was delivered on that dark and holy night. We remember the coming of the Light of the world.

responsibility tonight is to take care of a sick little lamb."

"Oh, papa, Basil is a chipmunk, not a sheep."

"Nonetheless… Would you have me watch the Christmas play while a baby is sad and crying in bed?"

My two youngsters reluctantly shook their heads.

I could see the conflict in Edmund's face. He knew that he was walking away from a priceless memory, a memory never to be recaptured. It was the one thing that could cause his doctor's

# PEACE ON EARTH

*Ideas for Christmas Eve*

- Read the Christmas story (Luke 2:1-20 and Matthew 2:1-23) by candlelight.
- Hang stockings.
- Shovel a neighbor's driveway on a snowy day.
- Deliver cookies to friends and neighbors.
- Attend a candle-lighting service at church.

- Join the chorus at a *Messiah* sing-along.
- Tour neighborhoods to view Christmas lights and displays.
- Watch Frank Capra's movie *It's a Wonderful Life*.
- Pray for peace in the world.
- Take a long winter's nap.

45

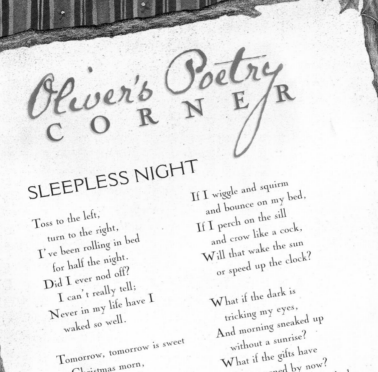

# Oliver's Poetry CORNER

## SLEEPLESS NIGHT

Toss to the left,
 turn to the right,
I've been rolling in bed
 for half the night.
Did I ever nod off?
 I can't really tell;
Never in my life have I
 waked so well.

Tomorrow, tomorrow is sweet
 Christmas morn,
The best day of all,
 about to be born,
But the night chugs along
 like a long, black train,
With cars full of stars
 in a moonlit chain.

If I kick off my covers
 and stand on my head,

If I wiggle and squirm
 and bounce on my bed,
If I perch on the sill
 and crow like a cock,
Will that wake the sun
 or speed up the clock?

What if the dark is
 tricking my eyes,
And morning sneaked up
 without a sunrise?
What if the gifts have
 been opened by now?
Would they leave me in bed
 and forget me somehow?

Would they, could they,
 forget about me?
Come along, blankie,
 we'll sleep by the tree!

# HOLLY POND HILL GAZETTE

**Dear Primrose,**

Our neighbors happen to be squirrels and you know all about squirrels. They never cease chattering. Well, the neighbor girl, little miss chatterbox extraordinaire, just informed my daughter that Santa Claus doesn't exist. Can you imagine? On Christmas Eve, no less! Now my poor daughter is in hysterics. She doesn't know whom to believe, a squirrel or her own mother. She won't even leave out the cookies and milk. Whatever shall I do?

Yours sincerely,
Mightily Mortified

**Dear Mightily Muffed,**

I suppose you knew this was bound to happen sooner or later. Your daughter would eventually observe that reindeer lack the necessary appendages to fly. And besides, your chimney is much too small to accommodate a jolly round elf.

Every year readers ask the same question, "What should I tell my children about Santa Claus?" There seem to be two opposing camps. In the one camp are parents who frown upon everything Santa. These parents reason that Santa has become the department stores' substitute for the Christ child and that all this North Pole business is a falsehood. In the other camp, there are parents who delight in the fairy tale and who go to great lengths to keep Santa alive, even when the fake beard falls off, so to speak.

I think a little dose of the Golden Rule is in order here. Why not tell your children what you expect your children to tell you—the truth? Tell your children from the get-go that Santa Claus is a fairy tale and that elves are all make-believe. Then you are free to enjoy the North Pole for all it's worth.

Is playing make-believe any less magical simply because it's make-believe? Not in the least. Children love to play princess and pirate even though they know they don't live in a castle or sail on a galleon. By all means have fun with Santa Claus and all the trappings. So long as you don't depart from the truth, your children will enjoy the fairy tale and have nothing to unlearn. At the same time, your child will be less inclined to doubt your word when you share about the One who is our real reason for celebrating Christmas.

Don't forget to tell your children the age-old legends about Saint Nicholas, who was indeed a real person. Share with them how Saint Nicholas was generous and jolly because he loved God.

My advice, dear reader, is to come clean with your daughter. Tell her the truth so as not to prolong the agony. Then the two of you can enjoy the cookies and milk yourselves!

Meticulously yours,
Primrose Lapin

# HOT CHOCOLATE AND HOT VANILLA

The cacao bean is one of the culinary wonders of the world, but chocolate has been a Christmas staple for only a hundred years or so. The original hot chocolate, Aztec style, was a bitter beverage flavored with cornmeal and chili peppers. Today's Mexican hot chocolate usually contains bittersweet chocolate, frothy hot milk, and cinnamon.

For the Boxwood family, hot chocolate is a special drink reserved for the Christmas season through Epiphany on January 6. We usually make a batch whenever the snow flies. Because we don't drink hot chocolate any other time during the year, it has become a much-loved holiday tradition. Here are some variations you're sure to enjoy. The base of each recipe is a sweetened, unflavored hot chocolate mix, prepared as directed.

## CREAMY RUM CHOCOLATE

For every mug of hot chocolate, stir in 1 tablespoon of warm, sweetened condensed milk and 1/4 teaspoon of rum-flavored extract. Add a layer of mini marshmallows.

## COOL MINT HOT CHOCOLATE

For every mug of hot chocolate, stir in 1/8 teaspoon of peppermint extract or 1 teaspoon of peppermint syrup. Serve with a peppermint candy cane.

## MIDNIGHT CHOCOLATE

For every mug of hot chocolate, stir in 1 tablespoon of dark chocolate syrup. Sprinkle with dark chocolate shavings. For a black forest flavor, add a splash of maraschino cherry juice.

## HOT BUTTERSCOTCH CHOCOLATE

For every mug of hot chocolate, add 1 tablespoon of sweetened condensed milk, 1 teaspoon of melted butter, and 1/4 teaspoon of butterscotch extract. Serve with a butterscotch candy cane.

## HOT MOCHA CHOCOLATE

For every mug of hot chocolate, add 1 teaspoon of instant coffee or 2 teaspoons of coffee syrup.

## HOT VANILLA

Vanilla lovers, this is the perfect alternative to chocolate. For every cup of hot milk, add 1/4 teaspoon vanilla flavor, 1 teaspoon of honey, and a sprinkling of ground cinnamon. Serve with a stick of cinnamon bark.

# REJOICE GREATLY

I should be sorry, my lord, if I have only succeeded in entertaining them;
I wished to make them better.

—HANDEL TO LORD KINNOULL

AFTER THE FIRST LONDON PERFORMANCE OF *MESSIAH*, MARCH 1743

When I first heard Handel's *Messiah*, with its powerful arias and grand choruses, I felt as if a glorious fire had been kindled in my breast. Now that I have heard the oratorio many times through, its familiar notes have become a comfort music to me.

We think of Handel's *Messiah* as Christmas music, but it actually encompasses the whole gospel message, from the Old Testament prophecies to the Last Judgment. I resist the urge to listen to it outside of Yuletide, however, as I love identifying *Messiah* with the most wonderful time of the year.

- Handel composed *Messiah* in only 24 days.
- After finishing the "Hallelujah" chorus, Handel supposedly wept and said to his manservant, "I did think I did see all Heaven before me and the great God Himself."

- When King George II first heard the "Hallelujah" chorus, he was so awed that he rose to his feet and, of course, his subjects followed. Ever since that performance, audiences have stood during the "Hallelujah" chorus.
- Handel was mainly a composer of operas before he turned his attention to oratorios.

Another magnificent oratorio, by no means to be neglected, is Johann Sebastian Bach's *Christmas Oratorio*. This masterpiece, completed in 1735, preceded *Messiah* by seven years.

# God Bless Us, Everyone!

## CELEBRATING CHRISTMAS DAY

Awake, glad heart! get up and Sing,
It is the Birth-day of thy King!
—HENRY VAUGHAN

I'm in the middle of a sweet dream when the chiming of the grandfather clock awakens me. Five o'clock. I hear the patter of little feet coming down the hall.

"It can't be Christmas morning," Edmund mumbles. "It's too dark outside."

"Ssssssh," I tell him. "I'm still asleep."

The little feet pause outside of our bedroom door. Edmund pretends to snore loudly. I hear whispers and giggles and then the little feet go creaking down the stairs.

"Tea," Edmund groans. "I cannot move until there's a whiff of breakfast tea in the air. Do you suppose our children will brew us a pot?"

"You're still dreaming, dear."

"But it can't be morning," Edmund insists. "There isn't a speck of daylight outside."

We hear the squeals of delight downstairs and then the crunchings of candy canes. Ribbons are torn from the sweetmeat boxes. In our home, the children are welcome to any treat they find on the Christmas tree. We deliberately hang up a few surprises the night before. The rules of the house, however, forbid peeking in stockings or opening presents until everyone has breakfasted.

As the happy noises grow louder downstairs, Edmund and I find ourselves wearing silly grins. I give him a peck on the cheek. "Merry Christmas, Santa," I say.

We Boxwoods are practically perfect Victorians on Christmas day. We share a light breakfast, usually cinnamon rolls and tea, and open presents. As the sun comes up, we walk to church for morning prayer.

The service is short, but the children are usually drowsy by the time we make our way home. Emily and Oliver take midmorning naps or play quietly with their new toys. Edmund and I meanwhile prepare for Christmas dinner, basting the Christmas roast (an enormous stuffed cabbage), stirring up the eggnog, and warming the mince pies.

We Boxwoods love to share our feast with family and friends, and typically invite enough guests to fill two tables. We begin dining promptly at half past twelve. The highlight of the meal is always the plum pudding, which we douse with brandy and set aflame.

After dinner, and once the china has been cleared, the fun begins. There is never a loss for things to do. We tear apart Christmas crackers. We listen to the children recite the poetry of Browning and Tennyson. Someone is certain to serenade us with the piano or a violin and there are always card tricks and hat tricks.

When it's time for charades, everyone

gathers in the parlor. We split up into two teams and take turns miming the titles of books and dramas. But we don't stop with charades. We also play Blind Man's Bluff, Foxes and Geese, and a host of other games. As the evening wears on, we take up places around the fire and listen to tall tales and stories of daring adventures. Around midnight we play one last game—Yawning for Cheese—before everyone reluctantly takes his leave.

Whenever possible, we Boxwoods share our festivities with folks who are far from home on Christmas. We affectionately call them "strays." Sometimes our strays will be foreign students from the nearby college.

I can remember one Christmas when a foreigner made a beautiful difference in our family celebration. We had been having a rather dreary Advent overall. Early in the season we toppled like dominoes to a horrid influenza and, though we decked the halls as usual, none of us had really caught the holiday spirit. Even on Christmas morning, with cinnamon rolls browning in the oven, none of us were especially thrilled to be entertaining that afternoon.

It was quarter to seven when we heard a loud knock at the front door. Oliver immediately bounced away to investigate. The next thing I heard was the shout, "Happy greetings!" in the vestibule.

"Mom? Dad?" Oliver called uncertainly.

As it turns out, it was our foreign guest, a young sea otter, who had just arrived with a steaming bowl of sea urchin paella in hand. "Merry season!" he shouted when we all had assembled about him. Edmund hastened to help him off with his coat while I shook his hand and bid him "merry season" in return. None of us had the heart to tell him that he was five hours early.

When we led him into the parlor to offer him a chair, he let out a gasp of delight. He walked over to our tree with his arms outstretched, as if he were going to hug it. Instead he clapped his hands. "Is a very very best tree," he said. "I like it most good of everything!"

> Evenings we knew,
> Happy as this;
> Faces we miss,
> Pleasant to see.
> Kind hearts and true,
> Gentle and just,
> Peace to your dust!
> We sing round the tree.
>
> —WILLIAM MAKEPEACE
> THACKERAY

The sea otter sat down for a moment, but for a moment only. He spied our nativity scene and was back on his feet, eager to study it more closely. When the children let him pick up the figurines, a big smile spread on his face from ear to ear. Edmund and I explained to him the meaning of the scene and why it was the most cherished decoration in the house.

Well, that started a grand tour of all the rooms. We showed our guest the Advent wreath (with the burning Christ candle), the holly garlands, the stockings, the kissing ring, the Christmas card display, and the wassail bowl.

Somehow, as we explained to him about all of our customs, with the children chiming in, the joy of Christmas began stealing over us. All the things we take for granted, the many familiar touches of the season, presented themselves to us in the fullness of their beauty. What a wonderful life we are privileged to live! By the time we finished the tour, we were all in a fine humor and fit to be merry.

"And now is time for peekneek?" the sea otter asked.

> It is good to be children sometimes and never better than at Christmas.
> —CHARLES DICKENS

"Peekneek?" asked Oliver.

"I think he means picnic," said Emily.

"Yes, yes, peekneek. In this country, you have peekneeks, no? I learn about these in my books."

"I don't think you'd fancy eating outside on a snow drift," Edmund said.

"Yes, yes. I make paella for peekneek."

"Permit me to rephrase myself. I don't think I'd fancy it, to be perfectly honest."

"Edmund," I said, suddenly struck with an idea. "Why don't we spread out a blanket on the floor in the parlor? We could picnic under the Christmas tree."

"My dear, you are one smart cookie!"

And so we did. We lit every taper on the tree and there, in the middle of the parlor, we sat down to rolls and tea. Not only were we all beaming with holiday cheer, but thanks to our guest we started a new tradition—picnicking under the tree—a tradition that has been a part of our Christmas morning ever since.

# MERRY CHRISTMAS
*Ideas for Christmas Day*

- Enjoy mince pie or plum pudding.
- Tear apart a Christmas cracker.
- Hold a scavenger hunt for a family gift.
- Build a snowman.
- Take a brisk walk after dinner.
- Read *The Little Match Girl* and *The Fir Tree* by Hans Christian Andersen.
- Play charades.
- Recite Christmas poetry.
- Put a jigsaw puzzle together.
- Take a family photo.
- Sponsor a child through Compassion International or World Vision.

# VICTORIAN CHRISTMAS GAMES

*At Christmas play and make good cheer,*
*For Christmas comes but once a year.*

—THOMAS TUSSER

Nowadays, so many creatures spend a forgettable Christmas in front of the television or napping at the movies. Boredom does not have to be your fate on Christmas Day! After the dinner dishes are cleared, let the fun and games begin! It's during game time that long-lasting Christmas memories are made. All that's needed is a goodly mix of adults and children who are willing to set bashfulness aside.

The games suggested here were popular with the Victorians, who were such great gamesters that they often played until well past midnight. Their parlors were formal sitting rooms for most of the year, with barely any traffic, but on Christmas they became center stage for tomfoolery of every sort.

## BLIND MAN'S BLUFF

Many variations exist for this old favorite.

*The Classic Game:* One player is designated the blind man and a blindfold is tied over his eyes. The other players spin the blind man around and around until he is thoroughly disoriented. Standing in a wide circle around the blind man, the players take turns tapping him on the shoulders while the blind man gropes about trying to guess the identities of the tappers or the people he grabs. When the blind man guesses a player correctly, that player must take his place.

*Search the Room:* Having been spun about, the blind man must count slowly to five and then call out "Freeze!" The other players take up positions around the room and are forbidden to take any steps after the call to freeze. The blind man must find a replacement by groping about the room. The first player he touches becomes the new blind man. Players may contort themselves to avoid the hands of the blind man as long as they don't take any steps.

## FOXES AND GEESE

This is a game of tag for a snowy day outdoors. Choose an open space with plenty of fresh, untrampeled snow. One person should prepare the field by tramping down a big circular path in the snow, being careful not to step outside of the path. Next an X is tramped in the center of the circle, rim to rim, like the spokes of a wheel. The field is now ready for the other players. Appoint one person to be the fox. The other players automatically become geese. The fox must chase the geese along the paths of the snow-wheel. Under no circumstances may any player leave the paths. Whenever a goose is tagged, that goose becomes the fox and the old fox becomes a goose. The center of the circle, where the two diameters meet, may be used as a resting-place for geese. All geese must fly from the resting place if the fox says, "Fly away goose, fly away gander; Here's the fox, red with dander."

## THE MINISTER'S CAT

Although rabbits have few dealings with cats, this word game is a perennial favorite in Holly Pond Hill. Players sit in a circle and slap their knees in unison to create rhythm. Adjectives are used

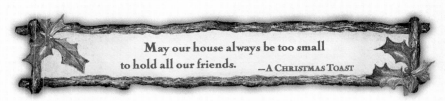

> **May our house always be too small
> to hold all our friends.** —A Christmas Toast

to describe the minister's cat, starting with A and ending with Z. For example, the lead person might say, "The minister's cat is an agile cat." The next person clockwise might say, "The minister's cat is an angry cat" or "The minister's cat is an awful cat." The A adjectives continue around the circle until the game returns to the leader. The leader then begins with a B adjective—"The minister's cat is a bumbling cat" or a "bombastic cat"—and so on through the alphabet. Adjectives may not be repeated or invented.

### SHADOW BLUFF

This game works best at a large party where there are plenty of identities to guess. Hang up a white sheet or tablecloth with a bright light shining on it. On one side of the sheet a guesser sits down and on the other side of the sheet (the side with the light) the players form a line. The room lights are turned off and the guesser must guess the identities of the players as they pass by the sheet in silhouette. The player may use wigs, pillows, and other items to fool the guesser.

### YAWNING FOR CHEESE

At the end of a game-filled Christmas Day, preferably in the wee hours of the night, gather all players together for one last hurrah. With everyone seated around in a circle, see who can yawn the loudest, the longest, the strangest, or the silliest… To the winner goes a chunk of fancy cheese. Snoring may be substituted for yawning.

# FOR THE BIRDS

On this day of sharing, don't forget our fine-feathered friends. Birds will flock to edible tree ornaments, especially in northern climes where food is in short supply during the winter. Hang these treats by string or ribbon from the branches of a small tree. With any luck you'll attract bright-feathered birds such as cardinals and evening grosbeaks. A flock of red-birds can decorate a tree like living Christmas ornaments.

Remember to use unsalted pretzels or low-salt peanut butter. On very cold days, even where there is plenty of snow, birds may be thirsting for a drink of water. Too much salt can lead to dehydration.

## BAGEL WREATH

Toast plain bagels, fresh or stale, until golden brown. Coat both sides generously with natural, low-salt peanut butter. Press coated bagels into bird-seed mix. Chill in freezer on wax paper before hanging by string or ribbons. If the weather outside is frightful (freezing temperatures), skip the freezer step.

## PRETZEL ORNAMENT

Melt suet in a saucepan. Using tongs, dip jumbo unsalted pretzels in suet until well coated. Cool in the refrigerator on wax paper. Press coated pretzels into a bowl of cornmeal. Hang by string or ribbon.

# EGGNOG

The word *eggnog* is supposedly a contraction of an item off tavern menus, "eggs 'n' grog." Here's a delicious eggnog recipe that calls for nary a drop of grog. It tastes much fresher than store-bought versions. While classic eggnogs were made from raw eggs, legitimate health concerns now necessitate cooking eggnog before chilling and serving. A candy thermometer will help you to get the temperature just right.

half gallon (2 quarts) low-fat milk
10 eggs
1/4 teaspoon salt
1 cup granulated sugar
1 teaspoon ground nutmeg
1 tablespoon rum-flavored extract

2 teaspoons vanilla extract
2 cups heavy cream

• In a Dutch oven or large saucepan, heat milk on low setting, taking care not to bring it to a boil. Boiling changes the flavor of milk and can cause a skin to form.
• In a large mixing bowl, beat eggs and salt together. Gradually add sugar and blend thoroughly.
• From the pan, transfer 2 cups of hot milk to the egg mixture. Beat milk and eggs until well blended. Add the egg mixture to the hot milk in the saucepan, stirring constantly.
• Continue to cook and stir over low heat until mixture thickens and reaches a "safe" temperature of 160° F. Cook and stir at this temperature for a minute or so.
• Remove eggnog from heat. Stir in nutmeg and extracts.
• Fill sink or bowl with ice. Place saucepan on top of the ice for 10 minutes to cool rapidly.
• Cover eggnog and refrigerate until

thoroughly chilled.
• Whip heavy cream until soft peaks form. Fold whipped cream into cold eggnog. Serve eggnog with a sprinkling of ground nutmeg. Keep unused portion refrigerated.

# Oliver's Poetry CORNER

## ODE TO A PRESENT

A gift for me!
What can it be?
Singin' rip the wrap with a snippety snap,
Thank you for my present!

I'll just give it a shake,
And hope it won't break,
Singin' toss the bow with a heigh and a ho,
Thank you for my present!

So much excitement in this shiny box,
Thank you, thank you for this...
pair of socks?!
Singin' bees with a sneeze, next present please!

# Holly Pond Hill GAZETTE

**Dear Primrose,**

Last Christmas, much to my chagrin, I received ear stockings and a set of ear-hair trimmers. Now I suppose that these are fine gifts in their own tactless way, but they were not at all what I was hoping for. In fact, I could barely conceal my disappointment as I tore off the wrapping paper. What is the proper response to a horribly thoughtless gift?

Sincerely,
Pity Party

**Dear Party Pooper,**

There is no such thing as a thoughtless gift. All gifts, however unwelcome, took some time, thought, and effort. Your job is to ooh and aah and act delighted no matter how dashed your expectations. Of course, if you happen to be intimate with the giver, you may want to reeducate him or her with gentle hints over the course of the next year.

My advice is to avoid inordinate expectations on Christmas morning. As those pretty boxes and bags accumulate under the tree, they create a sense of excitement and anticipation that no mortal gift can deliver. I have always felt a little deflated after a welter of unwrapping gifts. Even when I receive what I want, I'm still disappointed. This is because no material thing can satisfy my heart's deepest longings.

Truly, my friend, no one can shop better for you than your own self. When it comes to receiving Christmas gifts from others, it really is the thought that counts. Have no expectation at all of material happiness on Christmas Day and perhaps you will be pleasantly surprised.

Meticulously yours,
Primrose Lapin

# THE JOY OF GIVING

*—JOHN GREENLEAF WHITTIER*

Somehow not only for Christmas
But all the long year through,
The joy that you give to others
Is the joy that comes back to you.

And the more you spend in blessing
The poor and lonely and sad,
The more of your heart's possessing
Returns to make you glad.